DISNEY

Sofia the First

The Royal Slumber Party

PaRRagon

Bath • New York • Cologne • Melbourne • Delhi
Hong Kong • Shenzhen • Singapore

Sofia and Amber are having a royal sleepover tonight!

"This is where we'll be sleeping," Amber says.

"The observatory? We'll sleep under the stars!" Sofia cries.

"It's a royal slumber party," Amber says. "Everything has to be amazing."

Sofia's two best friends, Ruby and Jade, are coming.
Amber is shocked. "You invited village girls? You are
a princess now, Sofia. You should only invite princesses
to royal parties!"

"But Ruby and Jade are fun!" Sofia tells Amber. "You'll see."

The royal herald's trumpet sounds. "They're here!" Sofia cries.

Amber's friends, Princess Hildegard and Princess Clio, step out of their coaches. Behind them are Jade and Ruby in an oxcart.

"I can't believe we're here!" Jade exclaims, hugging Sofia.

"We're so excited!" Ruby adds.

It's time for the party to start! The princesses change
into fancy nightgowns. Ruby and Jade giggle as they roll
their hair in pinecone curlers – just like they do at home.
"We're at a royal sleepover!" they chant, pulling Sofia
up to join their silly dance.

The other princesses stare at Ruby and Jade.
"What are they wearing?" Hildegard says.
"What are they doing?" Clio wonders.
Amber frowns. "Are those pinecones?"
Ruby hears her and dances over. "Do you want one?
We brought extras."

Amber marches over to Sofia. "Sofia! Pinecones are not part of a perfect princess slumber party."

Sofia is worried. She wants her new sister and her old friends to like each other.

"They can fit in," she says. "They just need a little help, that's all."

Sofia has a great idea. "How would you two like
a royal makeover?" she asks her friends.
Ruby and Jade squeal with excitement!
Baileywick and Sofia's woodland friends help out.
They fix the girls' hair and dress them in pretty gowns
and sparkling tiaras.

Sofia makes her friends cover their eyes. Then she leads them to a mirror. "Open your eyes," she says. Jade and Ruby gasp when they see themselves.
"I'm a princess!" Ruby exclaims.
"Me, too!" says Jade.

Now it's time for party activities.
First comes fan decorating.
  Ruby and Jade have fun, but their
fans don't look very princessy.

Next the girls play a game of Pin the Tail
on the Unicorn.
  "Ooh! Ooh!" Jade says. "Can I go first?"
  But Jade ends up nowhere
near the unicorn!

Then the girls watch Cedric, the royal sorcerer, put on a magic puppet show in the banquet hall. During the show James, Sofia's brother, arrives with a message for the girls.

"Prince James!" Jade and Ruby cry as they run to him. They're thrilled to see the friendly prince!

Jade and Ruby are so excited that they accidentally knock over the chocolate-milk fountain. Oops! Chocolate milk splashes on to Amber's nightgown. She is furious!

"We're so, so, so sorry!" Ruby says to Amber.

"So sorry," Jade adds.

Amber walks off in a huff while Sofia shakes her head sadly.

Baileywick hurries Jade and Ruby away to get cleaned up. Then James tells the girls it's time for some dancing in the throne room.

"Let's go," Amber says. "Maybe we can enjoy five minutes of our party without Sofia's friends making a mess."

"We're so, so, so sorry!" Ruby says to Amber.
"So sorry," Jade adds.
Amber walks off in a huff while Sofia shakes
her head sadly.

Baileywick hurries Jade and Ruby away to get cleaned up. Then James tells the girls it's time for some dancing in the throne room.

"Let's go," Amber says. "Maybe we can enjoy five minutes of our party without Sofia's friends making a mess."

Now Sofia is even more worried! She goes to find her friends.

"I want you both to fit in with the princesses," Sofia explains.

"We look just like them now, don't we?" Jade says.

"Yes," Sofia says. "But princesses don't talk as much, or laugh as loud, or make as much mess."

Jade frowns. "We were just having fun."

"We're sorry," Ruby adds quickly. "We'll try to act more like Amber and the other princesses."

"Thank you!" Sofia is relieved. Now she's sure everyone will get along!

Sofia and her friends join the other girls in the throne room. But Ruby and Jade don't know how to waltz. All they can do is stand there and watch the four princesses dance.

After a while they tell Sofia that they would like to go home.

"But you're finally fitting in!" Sofia cries. "And you're not embarrassing me!"

"I'm sorry if we talk too much and laugh too loudly for your fancy new friends," says Jade. "Maybe we shouldn't be friends any more!"

Ruby takes Jade's arm and together they rush out of the room.

"Don't worry about them," Hildegard tells Sofia. "You're with us now."

Sofia goes after her friends but finds her mother instead. "I was trying to help Jade and Ruby fit in," she explains, "but I just made them feel bad."

"A true princess treats people with kindness, Sofia," Queen Miranda says gently. "If someone is your friend, you should like them for who they are."

Sofia knows her mother is right. She runs outside and finds her friends just as they are about to leave.

"I'm sorry about the way I acted," she says. "Please let me make it up to you. We can have our own slumber party – just the three of us!"

Jade and Ruby think for a moment and finally agree to stay.

Soon Sofia and her friends are in her room, having
a great time. They laugh – loudly! They talk – a lot!
They roll pinecones in their hair and put tiaras on top.

Meanwhile, Amber and her friends go back to the observatory.

"Finally, it's just us princesses," Amber says.

"This is a perfect party," Hildegard agrees with a yawn.

There's a long silence. The princesses are really bored.

"You know," Clio says, "Sofia's friends were kind of fun."

A moment later, Amber and her friends knock
on Sofia's door.

"Um, do you have room for a few more princesses?"
asks Amber.

Sofia looks at Jade and Ruby. "What do you think?"

"The more, the merrier," Ruby says with a smile.

Sofia and Amber end up having the perfect sleepover
with friends – old and new!